WITHDRAWN

min dition

published by Penguin Young Readers Group

Text copyright © 2006 by KNISTER
Illustrations copyright © 2006 by Eve Tharlet
Original title: ... das verspreche ich dir
English text translation by Kathryn Bishop
Coproduction with Michael Neugebauer Publishing Ltd., Hong Kong.
Rights arranged with "minedition" Rights and Licensing AG, Zurich, Switzerland.

Published simultaneously in Canada.
Manufactured in Hong Kong by Wide World Ltd.
Typesetting in Nueva by Carrol Twombly.
Color separation by Fotoreproduzioni Grafiche, Italy.

Library of Congress Cataloging-in-Publication Data available upon request.
ISBN 0-698-40040-2
10 9 8 7 6 5 4 3 2 1
First Impression

For more information please visit our website: www.minedition.com

KNISTER

A Promise Is a Promise

with Pictures by Eve Tharlet

Translated by Kathryn Bishop

minedition

Many animals sleep a special kind of sleep
in winter. It is deep and long.
It's called hibernation.

When spring comes, it is time to wake up.

Bruno, a little marmot, felt rested and strong after his long winter sleep. He wanted to go out and see the big wide world.

He ran and played until he was tired.
Then he found a little hollow in the grass and
snuggled down for a nap.

And oh, what Bruno saw when he opened his eyes again!

A flower,
a beautiful flower, a Dandelion.
"Hello," said Bruno.
He felt his heart beating excitedly.

"Hello," said Dandelion,
shining as brightly
as the sun.

The two had a wonderful time together as they laughed and played.

And every day Bruno thought his flower was lovelier than the day before.

Dandelion loved it when they danced by the light of the moon, and when it was time to sleep Bruno looked after her.

Then one day Dandelion asked, *"Do you trust me?"*

"Of course I trust you," answered Bruno, a bit surprised.

"No matter what happens?" Dandelion wanted to know.

"No matter what happens," said Bruno.

"Then I want you to take a deep breath and blow as hard as you can. Everything will be just fine, I promise," said Dandelion.

So Bruno blew with all his might.

But something awful happened. What had he done?

He had ruined his flower. Bruno felt so sad.

"But she promised everything would be fine," said Bruno.

"And I promised to trust her. A promise is a promise!"

But what did Dandelion mean when she said,
"Everything will be just fine?"

He sighed and in a whisper said, "She promised."

Then he started out into the big wide world, alone.

Bruno had such fun discovering
so many new things.

How he wished he could tell
his flower.

And all the while he couldn't stop thinking about the promise. What did Dandelion mean when she said, *"Everything will be just fine?"*

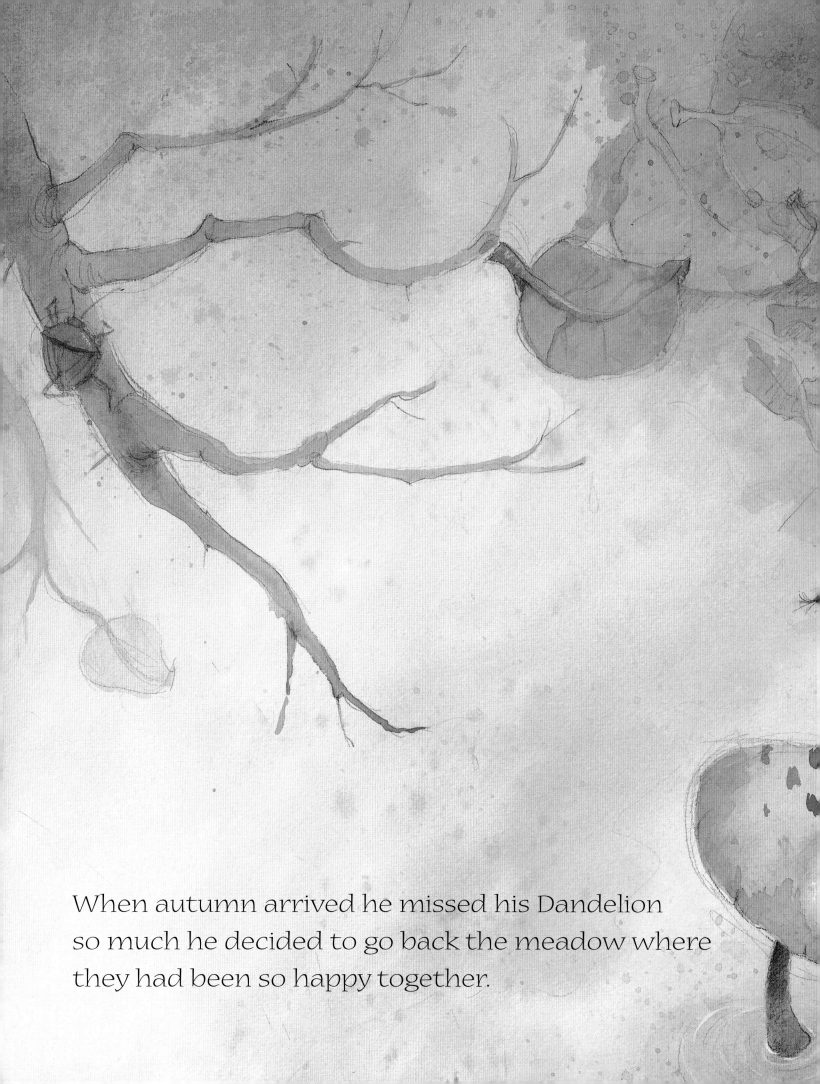

When autumn arrived he missed his Dandelion
so much he decided to go back the meadow where
they had been so happy together.

As the weather started getting colder,
Bruno started getting sleepy.
It was time, he thought, to build a den for
his long winter sleep.

He snuggled down and closed his eyes.

"A promise is a promise," he thought, and
Dandelion promised everything would be just fine.
And he fell into a deep, deep sleep.

When it was time for Bruno to wake up,
he opened his eyes and....

Oh, what a sight he saw!